S0-AVN-136

CHICKEN
LITTLE
and THE BIG BAD WOLF

I AM SO NOT SCARED OF ANY WOLF!

SAM WEDELICH

SCHOLASTIC INC.

I DON'T CARE _HOW_ BIG OR BAD HE IS!

BESIDES, I'VE NEVER EVEN _SEEN_ A WOLF!

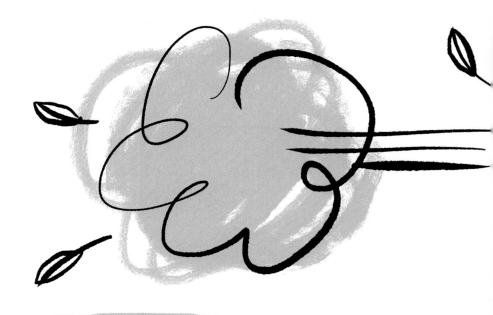

OH - NO
OH - NO
OH -
NO!

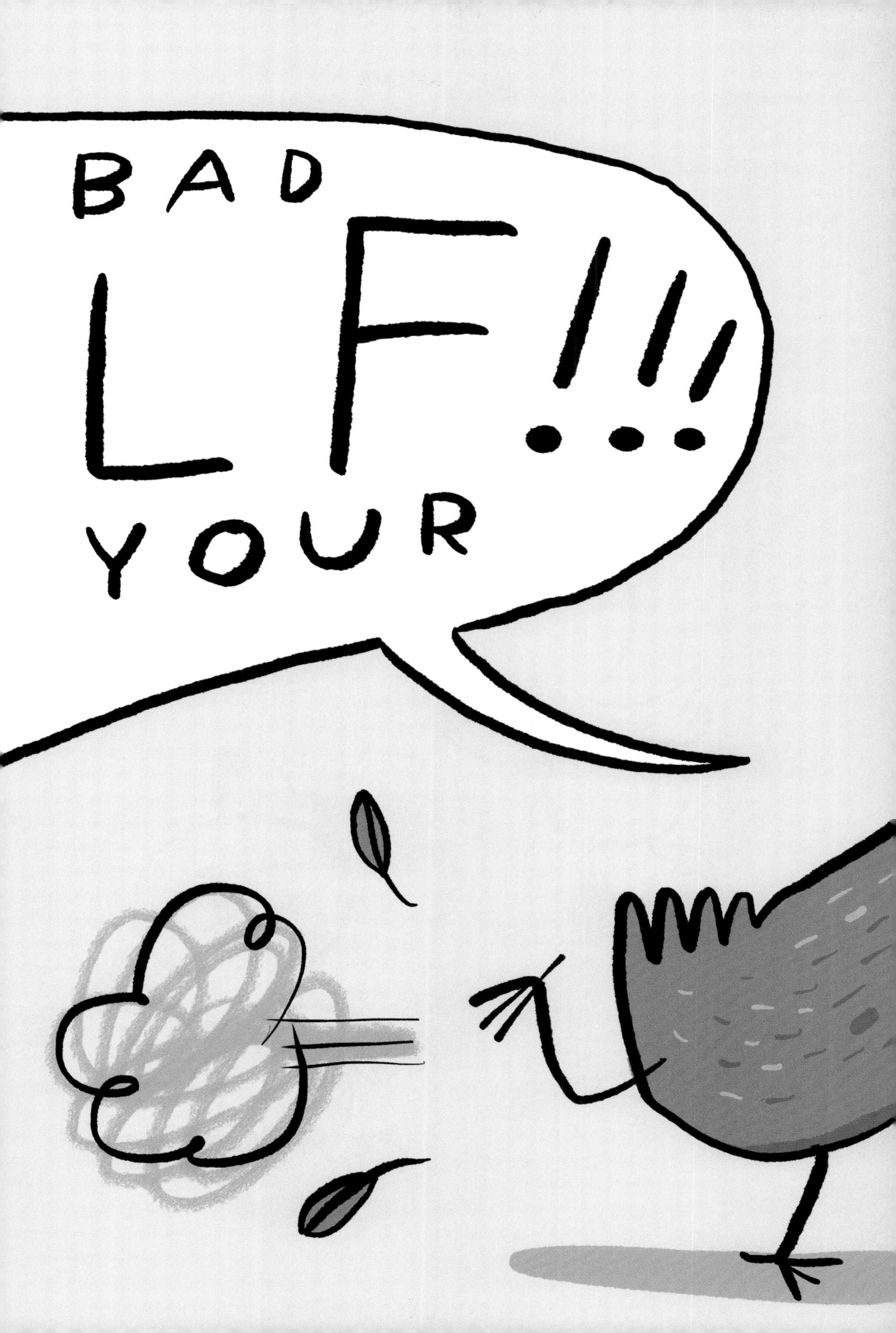
BAD LF!!! YOUR

THEY DIDN'T AGREE ON MUCH, EXCEPT THAT HATCHING A PLAN WAS MUCH HARDER THAN HATCHING EGGS!

ULTIMATELY, THEY DECIDED THEIR BEST OPTION WAS TO FLY THE COOP.

(BUT EVERYONE KNOWS CHICKENS AREN'T VERY GOOD AT FLYING!)

AND THEY WERE.

For anyone who's had to look for a place to belong . . .
and for all the flocks that welcomed them in.

Copyright © 2021 by Sam Wedelich • All rights reserved. Published by Scholastic Inc., *Publishers since 1920.* Scholastic and associated logos are trademarks and/or registered trademarks of Scholastic Inc. • The publisher does not have any control over and does not assume any responsibility for author or third-party websites or their content. • No part of this publication may be reproduced, stored in a retrieval system, or transmitted in any form or by any means, electronic, mechanical, photocopying, recording, or otherwise, without written permission of the publisher. For information regarding permission, write to Scholastic Inc., Attention: Permissions Department, 557 Broadway, New York, NY 10012. • This book is a work of fiction. Names, characters, places, and incidents are either the product of the author's imagination or are used fictitiously, and any resemblance to actual persons, living or dead, business establishments, events, or locales is entirely coincidental.

• • •

ISBN 978-1-338-74724-9 • 12 11 10 9 8 7 6 5 4 3 2 1   21 22 23 24 25 26 • Printed in the U.S.A.   40 • Originally published in hardcover by Scholastic Press, March 2021 • This edition first printing, November 2021 • Sam Wedelich's illustrations were created digitally. • The type was hand lettered by Sam Wedelich. • The set type is Amatic Regular. • The book was art directed and designed by Marijka Kostiw and edited by Tracy Mack.